# Disney

# DUMBO

Written by **CALLIOPE GLASS**

Illustrated by **DOMINIC CAROLA** and **RYAN FELTMAN**

centum

# ONCE UPON A TIME,

a ragged little circus rolled into a ragged little town.

The circus folk unpacked their gear and got to work.
Their cheerful racket echoed
as the striped tents went up.

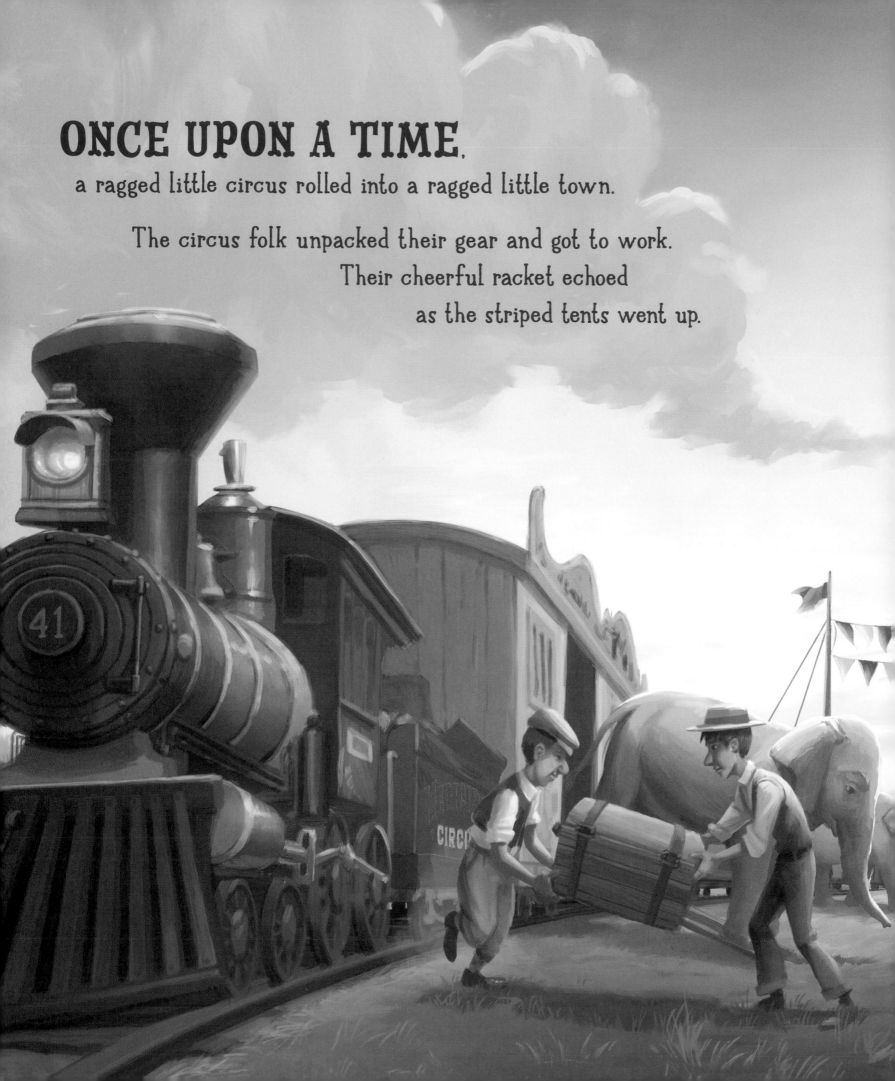

And at the heart of the hubbub ...
were a happy mama elephant and
her brand-new **BABY**.

But there was something **UNUSUAL** about this little one.

The baby's big ears made it hard for him to see.
The circus children, Milly and Joe, tried to teach him to blow
his ears off his face, but the little elephant accidentally snorted
a feather right into his trunk.

AH . . .

AH . . .

**ACHOO!**

Into the air he sailed – and for a moment, it almost looked as though he were flying! But then down to the ground he tumbled.

Soon the baby appeared in the circus for the very first time! Out he went, with his giant ears hidden.

But a feathered hat caught his eye, and ...

AH ...

AH ...

**ACHOO!**

Everyone could see the little elephant's giant ears.

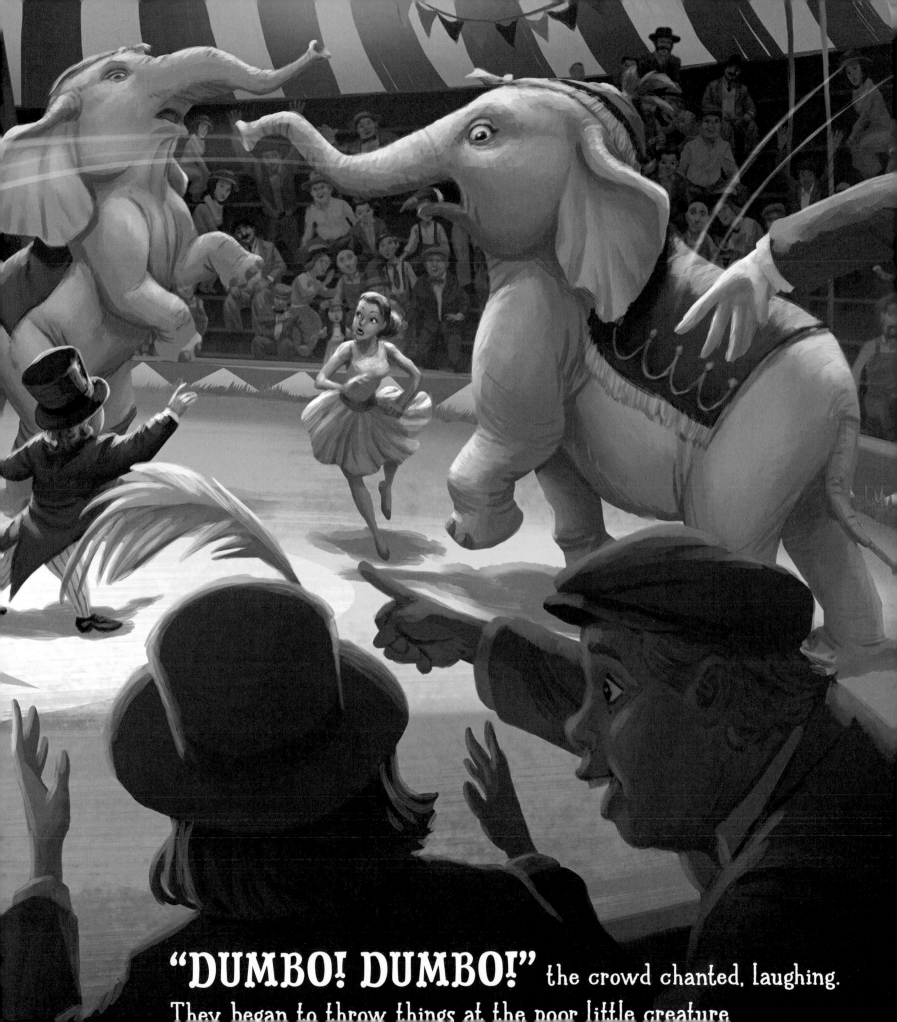

**"DUMBO! DUMBO!"** the crowd chanted, laughing.
They began to throw things at the poor little creature.

Dumbo's mama rushed in to save her baby —
and in all the panic, the circus tent fell down.

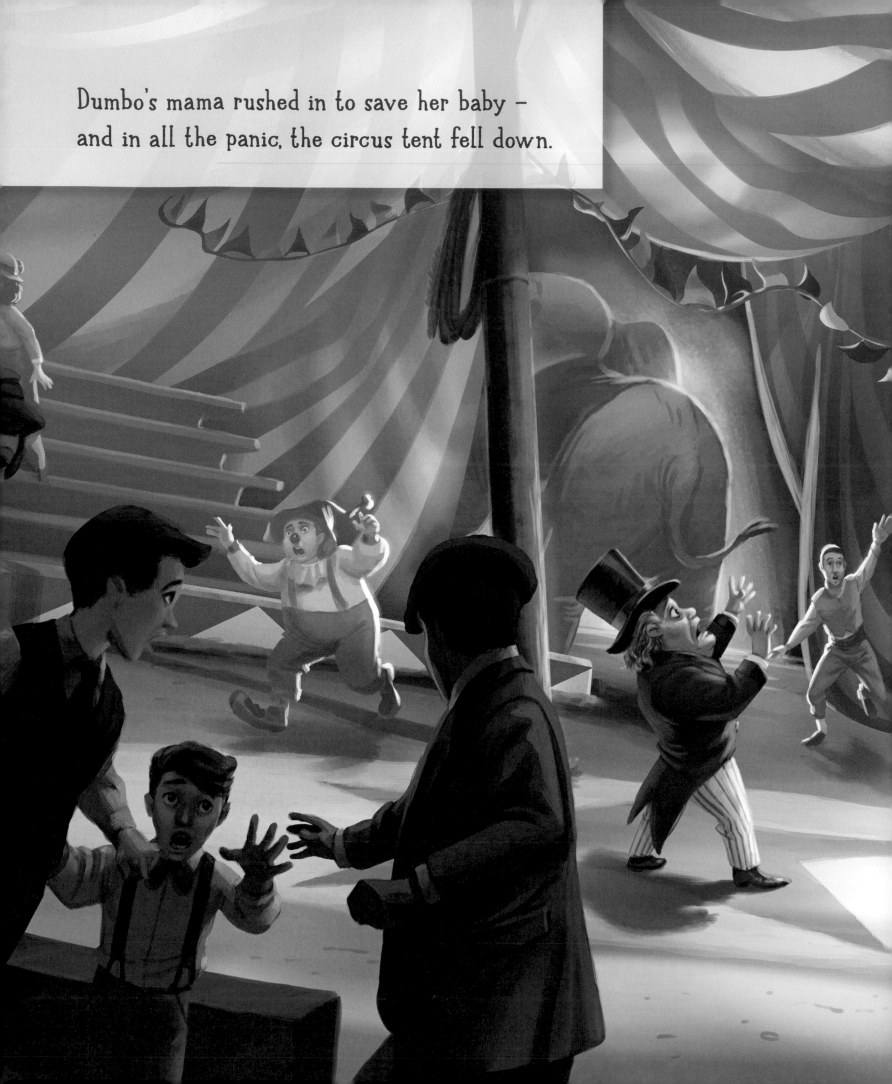

The tent was **RUINED.**
The stands were **RUINED.**
The circus was nearly **RUINED.**

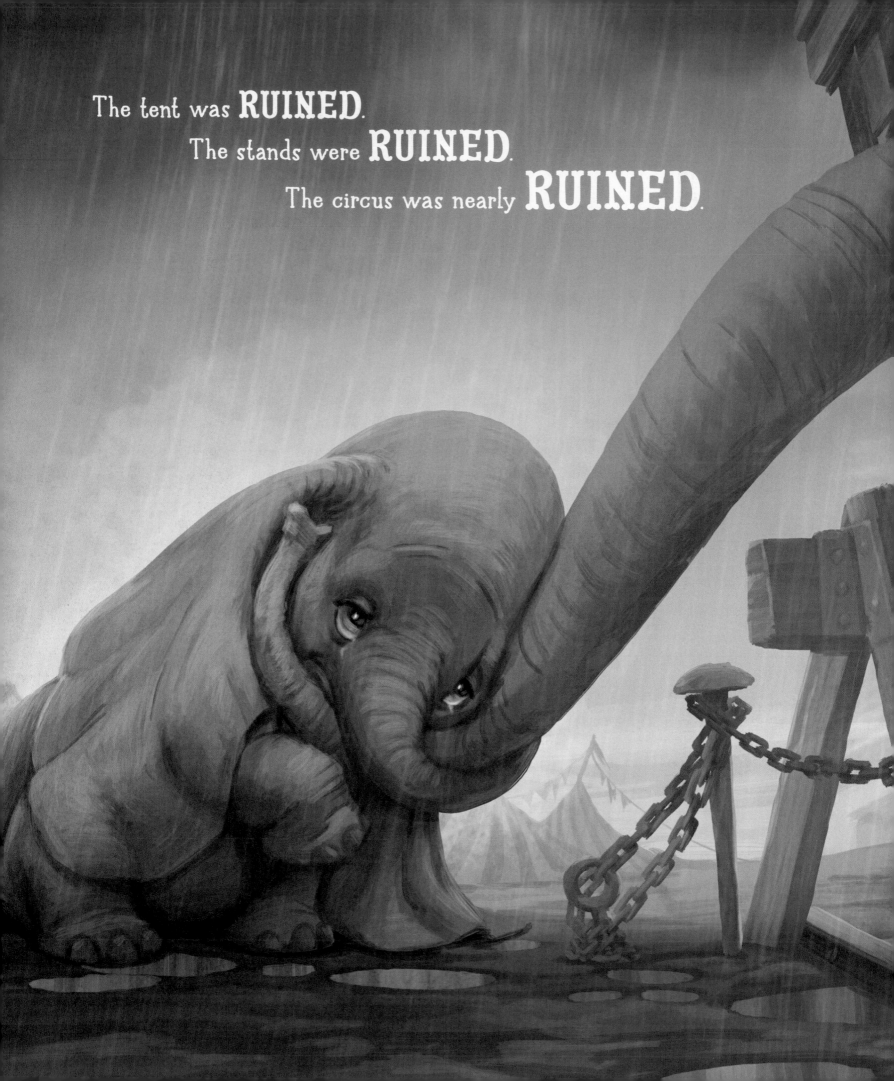

And Dumbo's mama was **LOCKED UP**.

The next day, Dumbo's mama was taken away.

# DUMBO
## WAS
### ALONE.

But he wasn't *all* alone. That night, Milly and Joe came to visit him.

It wasn't the same as having his mama.
But it was good to have friends.
Especially friends who brought peanuts ...
AND FEATHERS!

And once again: AH . . . . AH . . . .

Dumbo was flying – really and truly flying!

Finally, the circus was ready again. The tent was patched.
The tiered benches were rebuilt. And Dumbo was about to make history.

Maybe if he became a circus star, he could get his mama back.

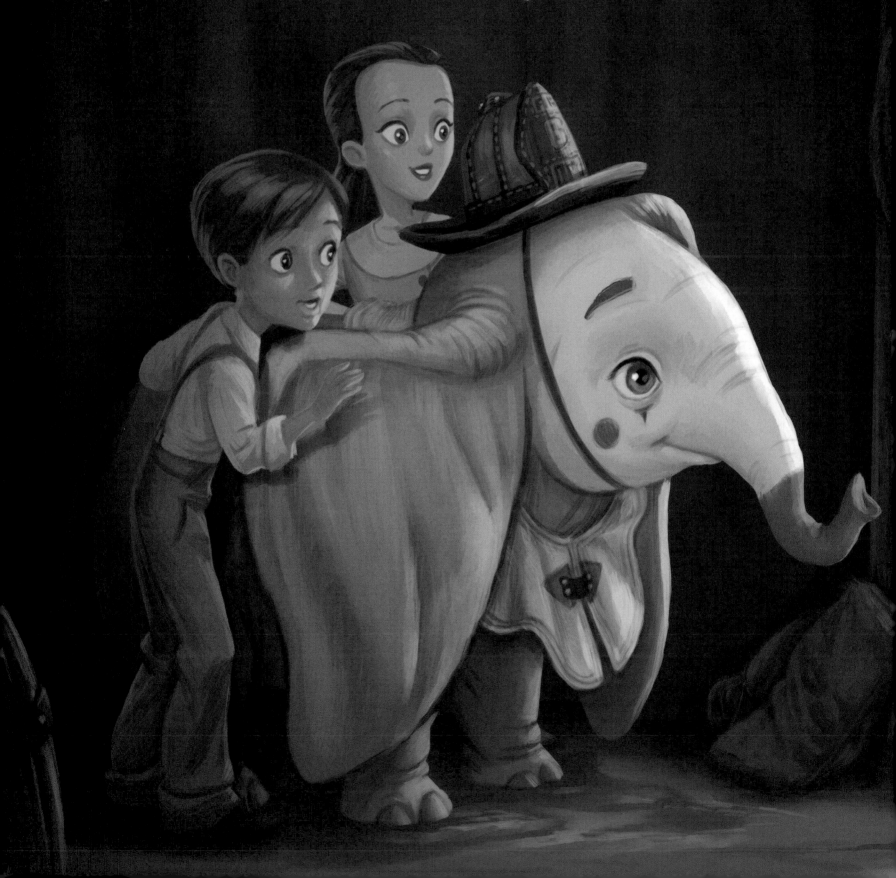

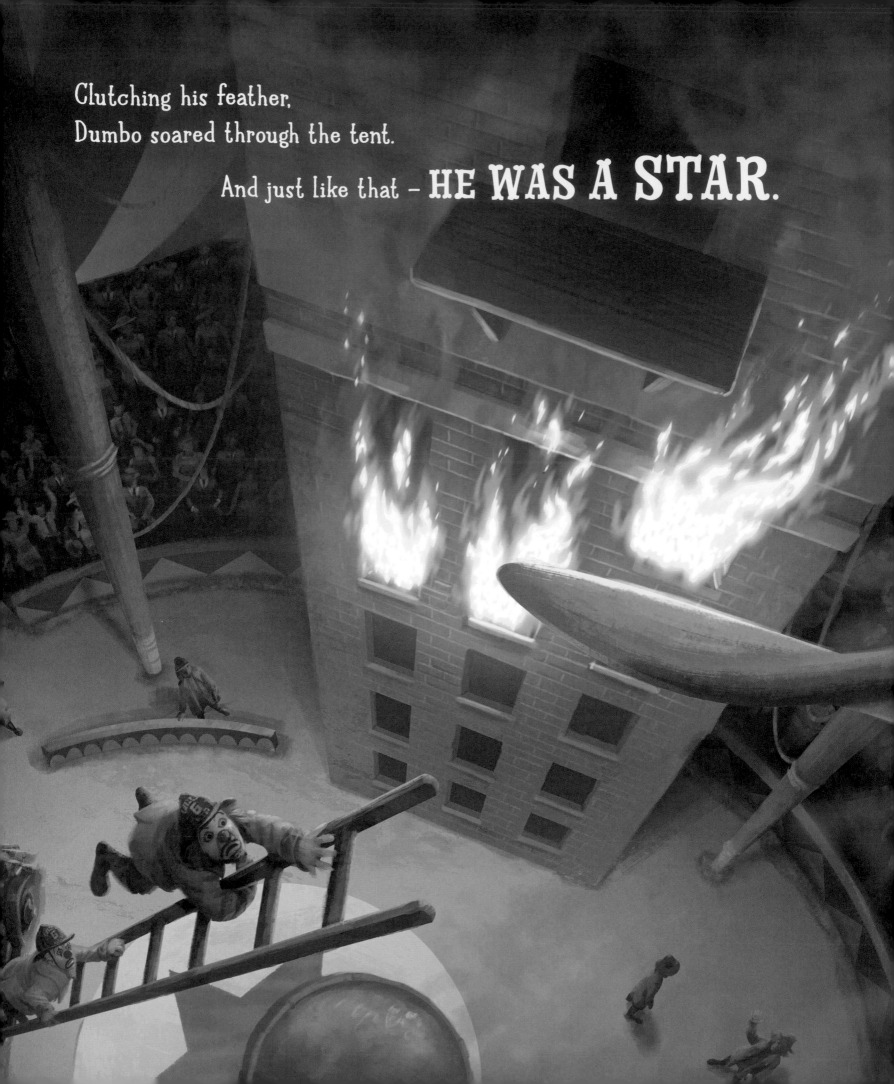

Clutching his feather,
Dumbo soared through the tent.

And just like that – HE WAS A STAR.

Soon Dumbo's ragged little circus was just as famous as he was. Too famous for a ragged little town – at least according to the big-time circus man V. A. Vandevere.

Before Dumbo and the children knew it, their ragged little circus had been bought by the big-time circus man.

And they were off to **NEW YORK –
TO DREAMLAND!**

The new tent was bigger. The new crowds were bigger.
And the new city was *much* bigger.

It made Dumbo feel even smaller.
He gave a frightened little cry.

And out in the night, someone heard that cry.
Someone who recognised it.
Someone who cried back.
MAMA!

Dumbo's mama was
also in Dreamland,
but locked up tight.
And yet, even through the thick bars,
Dumbo felt her love warming him.

Vandevere refused to let Dumbo's mama go. He thought Dumbo was better off *without* a mama.

But Dumbo didn't agree, and neither did the circus folk. The very next night, they staged

# A BREAKOUT!

Dumbo sailed through the sky.
On the ground, his mama
bumped along in a stolen truck.

# AND SOON –

Dumbo and his mama were reunited. Dumbo's friends understood the circus was no place for elephants – or any wild animals, for that matter. They helped Dumbo and his mama find a new home in the jungle.

And so, at last, and for good,

# THE VERY SPECIAL ELEPHANT AND HIS MAMA

lived happily — together and free.